Some words about maggots:

"Strike, Daisy! Strike!"
Uncle Clive

"Help help! I've been turned into a dog poo!"
An unlucky fisherman

"Duck!"
A duck

"Aaaaarrrrghhhh! There's a maggot in my tea!"
An angry river boater

"EEEEKKK!! There's something
wriggling in my pants!"
Jack Beechwhistle

"Oh my word, Daisy. What have you
done th...
Dais...

www.dais...

More Daisy adventures!

DAISY AND THE TROUBLE
WITH LIFE

DAISY AND THE TROUBLE
WITH ZOOS

DAISY AND THE TROUBLE
WITH GIANTS

DAISY AND THE TROUBLE
WITH KITTENS

DAISY AND THE TROUBLE
WITH CHRISTMAS

DAISY

and the TROUBLE with

MAGGOTS

by Kes Gray

RED FOX

DAISY AND THE TROUBLE WITH MAGGOTS
A RED FOX BOOK 978 1 849 41341 1

First published in Great Britain by Red Fox,
an imprint of Random House Children's Books
A Random House Group Company

This edition published 2010

3 5 7 9 10 8 6 4

Text copyright © Kes Gray, 2010
Cover illustration copyright © Nick Sharratt, 2010
Inside illustrations copyright © Garry Parsons, 2010
Character concept copyright © Kes Gray and Nick Sharratt, 2010

The right of Kes Gray, Nick Sharratt and Garry Parsons to be identified as
the author and illustrators respectively of this work has been asserted
in accordance with the Copyright, Designs and Patents Act 1988.

The Random House Group Limited supports the Forest Stewardship Council (FSC),
the leading international forest certification organization. All our titles that are printed
on Greenpeace-approved FSC-certified paper carry the FSC logo. Our paper
procurement policy can be found at www.rbooks.co.uk/environment

Mixed Sources
Product group from well-managed
forests and other controlled sources
www.fsc.org   Cert no. TT-COC-2139
© 1996 Forest Stewardship Council
FSC

Set in Vag Rounded

Red Fox Books are published by Random House Children's Books,
61–63 Uxbridge Road, London W5 5SA

www.daisyclub.co.uk

Addresses for companies within The Random House Group Limited
can be found at: www.randomhouse.co.uk/offices.htm

THE RANDOM HOUSE GROUP Limited Reg. No. 954009

A CIP catalogue record for this book is available from the British Library.

Printed and bound in Great Britain by
CPI Bookmarque, Croydon, CR0 4TD

To Mr Crabtree

CHAPTER 1

The **trouble with maggots** is they are too wriggly. If maggots weren't so wriggly, then what happened yesterday, when I went fishing with my Uncle Clive, would never have happened at all.

It's not my fault maggots are so wriggly.

Or tiggly.

Maggots are about the wriggliest, tiggliest things in the world. Especially when you shoot them through the air with a fishing catapult.

Fishing catapults make maggots REALLY wriggle tiggle. And go a long way.

AND land in places where you were only kind of, but not actually definitely aiming for.

Especially when it's windy.

Well, sort of windy.

OK, not that windy.

Allright, not very windy at all.

But the sun was definitely shining in my eyes. Which meant I couldn't really see where I was aiming with the catapult.

WHICH ISN'T MY FAULT!

CHAPTER 2

Fishing is the BEST!

When my Uncle Clive asked me if I wanted to go fishing with him on Sunday, I didn't even know what fishing was!

I didn't even know what a maggot looked like!

Or a bait box!

Now I do.

Now I know loads about fishing. More than Jack Beechwhistle anyway.

And Harry Bayliss.

It was two Sundays ago that Uncle Clive asked me if I wanted to go fishing with him. He came over to our house with Auntie Sue, and said he had bought a new fishing rod and was busting to try it out.

That's the **trouble with new fishing rods**. They make you want to go fishing even more!

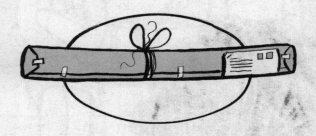

First of all he asked my mum if she thought I would like to go fishing with him. And then he asked my mum if she wanted to come too.

The **trouble with asking my mum if she wants to go fishing** is my mum doesn't really like fishing as much as me.

I don't know why, because fishing is absolutely brilliant!

Maybe she thought she'd have to touch the maggots!

Anyway, it didn't really matter,

because my Auntie Sue doesn't like fishing as much as me and Uncle Clive either. But she does like picnics! And so does my mum!

So that's what we did! We went FISHING AND PICNICKING all together at the same time!! Picnics and fishing go really well together. Especially if it's a nice hot summery day like yesterday was!

And especially if you go to the river at Paper Mill lock where all the river boats are!

CHAPTER 3

The **trouble with river boats** is Jack Beechwhistle thinks he knows everything about them.

When I went to school last Monday, I couldn't wait to tell Gabby I was going to be going fishing with my Uncle Clive. Trouble is, Jack Beechwhistle was listening when I told her.

That's the **trouble with Jack Beechwhistle**. He's got ears the size of an elephant.

Jack Beechwhistle thinks he knows

everything about rivers. Especially river boats.

Just because he goes to Paper Mill lock on Sundays to do canoeing lessons, he thinks that makes him an expert on everything in the whole world.

Jack Beechwhistle says he's canoed past loads of river boats, which definitely makes him an expert

on them. PLUS, he said being the captain of his own boat makes him a double expert.

Me and Gabby said that a canoe wasn't a type of boat at all, because it didn't have an anchor. Plus proper boat captains wear hats.

But Jack Beechwhistle said he did wear a hat when he was canoeing. It was a special safety hat, like a crash helmet, with straps that did up and everything. And he wore a life jacket.

Jack Beechwistle said that life jackets and canoe hats were better than captains' hats any day.

Then he said he knew more about fishing than me too!

And ducks.

So I called him a Poopy Face.

But he didn't listen.

He just kept telling me about fishing.

Jack Beechwhistle says he has canoed past loads of people when they were fishing. Which means he knows all about fishing AND river boats and everything. Which makes him a TRIPLE DIPPLE expert.

So I said he was a triple dipple Poopy Head.

But he didn't listen AGAIN!

Even with those great big elephant ears he didn't listen!

So I ignored him for the total rest of the day.

CHAPTER 4

When I asked my mum if a canoe was a proper type of boat, she said that it was. Even if it didn't have an anchor.

Which made me really cross.

Then she told me that it was wrong to call people triple dipple Poopy Heads, or even single dingle Poopy Heads. So I should say sorry to Jack Beechwhistle when I saw him at school the next day!

Which made me even crosser!

I was still feeling cross when I woke up on Tuesday morning.

I was cross when I got dressed.

I was cross when I had my breakfast.

I was cross when I cleaned my teeth.

I was cross when I put my packed lunch into my school bag.

And I was still cross when I got to school.

So there was no way I was going to say sorry to Jack Beechwhistle.

There was no way I was going to say ANYTHING to Jack Beechwhistle ever again!

But he made me.

He waited by the school gates with Harry Bayliss, and he made me talk to him. And listen to him.

So did Harry Bayliss.

The **trouble with Harry Bayliss** is he's a triple dipple Poopy Head as well.

He's only done about two canoeing

lessons, and he thinks he's an expert on fishing and river boats too!

When I saw Harry and Jack waiting by the school gates, I just knew they were waiting for me. And I just double knew they were going to tell me all about river boats and fishing AGAIN.

And guess what?

I was right.

I was right on Tuesday.

I was right on Wednesday.

I was right on Thursday.

And I was right on Friday too.

It made me SO CROSS!

CHAPTER 5

Guess what they told me on Tuesday. . .

They said that some fish have real actual teeth! Real actual teeth that can bite through fruit cakes.

The **trouble with Paper Mill lock,** is it's got a café that sells fruit

cake and everything. Harry Bayliss said if you dropped a slice of fruit cake into the river beside Paper Mill lock café, a fish with really big teeth would swim up and swallow it in one go.

Jack Beechwhistle said that if I wanted to catch a fish with big teeth out of Paper Mill river on Sunday, then I should absolutely definitely put a slice of fruit cake on my hook.

Then Harry Bayliss said I should try a chocolate mini roll, with the wrapper off.

But I didn't want to catch a fish with big teeth anyway.

I'd much rather catch a roach.

On Wednesday morning when I got to school, Harry Bayliss and Jack Beechwhistle were waiting outside the school gates again.

Guess what they told me this time.

They told me that once when they were canoeing in the big pool right by Paper Mill lock, they saw a canoe

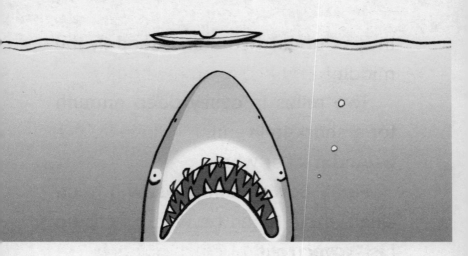

get eaten by a shark!

Luckily there wasn't anyone in it, otherwise the person driving the canoe would have been eaten too.

At first I didn't believe there were sharks living in Paper Mill lock, but then Jack Beechwhistle told me that the pool they do canoeing practice in was about two miles deep in the middle!

Two miles is easily deep enough for a shark to live in.

And a killer whale.

Harry Bayliss said he saw a huge killer whale when he was practising his "kayak rolls."

The **trouble with kayak rolls** is you have to do canoeing to know what they are.

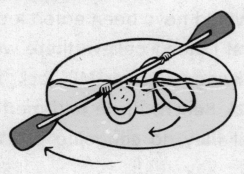

"Kayak" is another word for a canoe. And a 'kayak roll' is like a sideways roly poly in a canoe under the water. Jack Beechwhistle said you need to be an expert to do kayak rolls in a canoe.

Your head has to go under the water, your shoulders have to go under the water, everything sticking out of your canoe has to go right under the water, until you go all the way under in a circle and turn your canoe up the right way again.

Without dying.

Harry said that learning to do kayak rolls is really scary at first, because you think you're going to

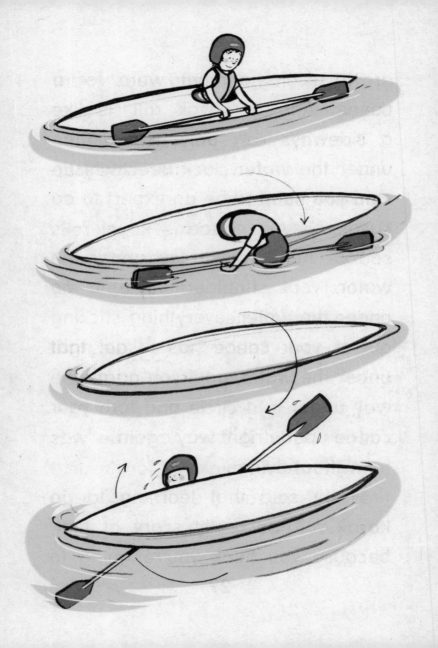

drown when your head goes under the water.

But after you come up the right way and you haven't died, you stop worrying so much.

I said if you asked me, kayak rolls sounded silly. I said if I was driving a canoe I'd stay the right way up in my canoe all the time.

But Jack Beechwhistle said that kayak rolls were super important.

Trouble is, he couldn't think why.

Harry said it was when he was trying to do a kayak roll for the first time that he saw the killer whale in Paper Mill pool.

He said he was upside down in his canoe, holding his breath and looking straight down below him, when this huge black and white shape loomed towards him out of the depths.

I said it might have been Free Willy, because Free Willy definitely escapes at the end of the film he's in, so who knows where he escaped to? Maybe he moved to Paper Mill lock?

But Harry said the killer whale he saw was MUCH scarier than Free Willy.

He said it had really starey eyes and red teeth, and that it licked its lips when it saw him.

That's the **trouble with killer whales.** If they're not Free Willy, they're probably going to eat you.

Luckily Harry still had his paddle in his hands. So he used it to bash the whale right between the eyes.

Harry says if you bash a killer whale between the eyes with a paddle, it will scare it away for certain.

Jack Beechwhistle said that if I

wanted to catch a killer whale or a massive shark when I went fishing with my Uncle Clive, I should definitely cast my bait into the middle of the pool at Paper Mill lock.

But I didn't want to catch a killer whale or a massive shark anyway.

I'd much rather catch a dace.

CHAPTER 6

When I got to school on Thursday, I thought Harry Bayliss and Jack Beechwhistle weren't there at first. Which was good, because I was getting really fed up with them being experts on fishing.

Trouble is, they were hiding behind the wall, waiting to jump out on me.

"Don't fish near the bridge whatever you do!" they said. "If you fish near Paper Mill bridge, the water troll might get you!"

"A water troll lives right under

Paper Mill bridge – didn't you know!" said Harry.

The **trouble with water trolls** is they eat fishermen. And fishergirls.

Or if they're not hungry, they make you into slaves.

Jack Beechwhistle said that one Sunday he was canoeing under Paper Mill bridge, when this giant hairy hand with webbed fingers came right up out of the water and tried to

grab him by the life jacket!!!

Luckily he had a whistle on his life jacket for emergencies, so he blew it, and the water troll was frightened away.

I said a troll would never be frightened away by a silly old whistle, but Jack said that the echo under the bridge made the whistle sound a hundred times louder.

Trolls don't like really loud whistles. Especially water trolls with webbed ears.

At first I didn't believe in water trolls, but then Jack Beechwhistle told me a really scary story about a little girl called Androlina who got captured by the actual water troll under Paper Mill actual bridge.

He didn't eat her though. He made her into his slave!

This is what Jack Beechwhistle said had happened.

Androlina was a seven-year-old girl who looked really really like me. She had the same hair as me, and the same

face as me and everything.

She lived in the village and was very poor. So one day, to earn some extra pocket money, she got a job doing a paper round, delivering newspapers and magazines to houses right by the river.

The **trouble with houses right by the river** is you can't cycle to them.

Because there are no roads to cycle on or anything. There's only river.

So instead of doing her paper round on her bike, Androlina had to do it in a canoe instead.

One day, in the really snowy winter, Androlina was canoeing towards Paper Mill  bridge, when her canoe struck an iceberg and sank!

That's the **trouble with icebergs**.
They sink everything.

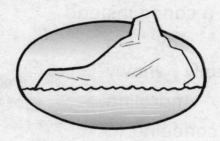

Trouble was, she still had loads
of newspapers and magazines to
deliver.

So she grabbed all the newspapers
and magazines before they could get
wet, held them up above her head,
and decided to swim to all the other
houses instead.

The **trouble with swimming**

under Paper Mill bridge is that's where the water troll lives.

The **trouble with swimming under Paper Mill bridge with both hands above your head** is it makes it really easy for a water troll to grab you.

So Androlina got GRABBED!

By WEBBED HANDS!!

WITH HAIRY WARTS ON!

But luckily the water troll had already eaten about eight people in canoes for breakfast.

So Androlina got made into an underwater slave for ever instead!!!

Harry Bayliss said that because I look just like Androlina, the water troll was bound to try and grab me too if I went near the bridge with my Uncle Clive on Sunday.

I said my Uncle Clive would save me, but Harry said that water trolls ate Uncle Clives for breakfast.

And dinner. And tea.

Jack Beechwhistle said maybe I should use myself as bait when I went fishing with my Uncle Clive. Then I could see if I could catch the water troll.

Then I could set Androlina free.

But I didn't really want to catch a water troll with my Uncle Clive.

I'd much rather catch a skimmer bream.

CHAPTER 7

By Friday I wasn't really sure I wanted to go fishing with my Uncle Clive any more.

I wasn't scared of the water troll or anything. It's just that when I found out about the underwater witch mermaid who lives at the bottom of Paper Mill river in a sunken haunted canal boat covered in cobwebs that don't dissolve, I kind of went off the idea of going fishing for a while.

Jack and Harry told me about the underwater witch mermaid. And the

spells she casts on people with her evil underwater fishing rod.

Jack Beechwhistle said she'd been living at the bottom of Paper Mill river ever since the Second World War.

That's when her canal boat got torpedoed by a submarine.

The **trouble with torpedoing and sinking a witch mermaid's canal boat** is, it makes the witch mermaid's powers eviller than ever.

Especially if her fishing rod turns into a wand with underwater haunted torpedo powers.

Harry Bayliss said that when the torpedo blew up the witch mermaid's canal boat, all the forces from the explosion went straight into the end of her fishing rod.

And her fingernails.

And her gumboils.

Which made her the powerfullest underwater witch in the world.

And crossest.

And ugliest.

And nastiest.

Apparently the underwater witch mermaid that lives at the bottom of Paper Mill river is so cross and so ugly and nasty, she turns fishermen into dog poos.

FOR NO REASON!!!!

That's what Jack Beechwhistle said.

And Harry Bayliss.

At first, I definitely didn't believe them, but Jack Beechwhistle swore on his Action Man's life that I would see actual dog poos on the actual riverbank at Paper Mill lock. Actual dog poos in the exact same places where the fishermen were standing when they got turned into dog poos by the witch's evil pooey spells.

Harry Bayliss said it was definitely true, and that sometimes if you put your ear right up close to some of the dog poos at Paper Mill lock, you can hear

Help!

the voices of the fishermen AND FISHERGIRLS trapped inside!

After that I went right off the idea of going fishing.

I went right off the idea of going fishing all through Friday morning assembly.

All through Friday morning lessons.

All through Friday morning break.

All through Friday lunch time. (I didn't even eat my cheese spread sandwiches.)

All through Friday afternoon lessons.

And all the way back to the school

gates, where my mum was waiting for me after school.

That was when Mum told me. . .

That HARRY BAYLISS AND JACK BEECHWHISTLE WERE LYING!

They'd been lying about EVERYTHING!!!

ALL WEEK!!!!!!!!!!!!!!!!!!!!!!!!

CHAPTER 8

The **trouble with liars** is they should be made to go to prison.

In fact, liars who tell lies about fishing like Jack Beechwhistle and Harry Bayliss should have to go to prison for about three hundred years.

And be made to eat peas every day.

Until they turn green . . . and their lips fall off.

When my mum told me that Harry and Jack had been winding me up about fishing ALL WEEK, I was so cross, I nearly kicked a lamppost.

Then, when my mum told me I was a Poopy Head for believing their silly stories in the first place, I DID kick a lamppost!

But then I wish I hadn't.

That's the **trouble with kicking lampposts**.

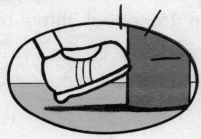

It really hurts.

My mum said she didn't think Harry or Jack knew the slightest thing about fishing. And if I wanted to know about fishing, then the only person I should be listening to is my Uncle Clive.

She said there were absolutely no sharks or whales or trolls or mermaids or water witches in Paper Mill river at all, and that if there were, she would use her magical Paper Mill picnic powers to fight them off.

She told me that Auntie Sue had a magic picnic hamper that had been given to her by a white wizard when she was a little girl.

Inside Auntie Sue's magic picnic hamper there were all the picnic weapons you could ever need to do battle on the riverbank with water trolls, water witches, water monsters or any other water baddies that came along when you were fishing.

Inside the hamper there were exploding sausage rolls, walkie talkie mini rolls, poison-gas sandwiches and a Thermos flask that fired long-range missiles.

Plus there was orange squash that made you invisible when you drank it.

And emergency boiled eggs that protected you with a force field when you peeled off the eggshell.

Except there wasn't.

Because now she was winding me up TOO!

That's the **trouble with mums after school.** They think they're SO funny.

WHEN THEY'RE NOT!

CHAPTER 9

I was still really really cross with Jack Beechwhistle and Harry Bayliss when I went to bed on Friday evening.

In fact I was so cross, I nearly didn't let my mum read me a bedtime story.

And I nearly didn't give her a goodnight kiss.

But I did in the end. Because bedtime stories and goodnight kisses are really important for my mum.

When I woke up on Saturday morning, I was kind of cross mixed with really excited.

By about just after breakfast, once my Coco Pops had gone down, I was mostly excited and hardly cross at all.

That's because I WAS GOING FISHING!

Not that day, the next day, but I was still really excited because even though it was only Saturday, I still had to get ready to go fishing!

The **trouble with getting ready to go fishing** is if you haven't been fishing before, you don't know what to wear.

I thought I would definitely have to wear wellies, but my mum said that as it was going to be such a hot day on Sunday, I would be better off wearing my trainers.

So I put my trainers by the front door.

"What trousers shall I wear?" I asked.

"Wear your oldest pair of jeans!" said my mum.

So I put my oldest pair of jeans by the front door.

"What T-shirt shall I wear?" I asked.

"Wear your green one with the yellow stripes," said my mum.

So I put my green T-shirt with the yellow stripes by the front door.

"What jumper shall I wear?" I asked.

"Take your red hoodie with the zip," said my mum, "just in case it gets chilly later."

So I put my red hoodie with the zip by the front door.

"What socks shall I wear?"

"You choose!" said my mum.

So I put my favourite football socks on the pile beside the front door. Plus two pairs of trainer socks in case it got chilly later.

Then I added my wellies just in case I fancied a paddle.

And the red bucket from the shed to put the fish in!

The **trouble with putting a pair of wellies, a bucket from the shed, a pair of trainers, a pair of jeans, a T-shirt, a red hoodie and three**

pairs of socks in a pile by the front door is when someone rings the doorbell, the door gets wedged when you try and open it.

Because your pile of fishing things is in the way.

At first, when I pulled the door back, it opened a little bit, but then one of my wellies folded over and got jammed underneath.

Then my bucket handle sort of got stuck underneath the hood of my hoodie.

And then the belt of my jeans got jammed around the bucket handle.

Which wasn't my fault.

It was the postman's fault really, because if he had put our letters through our letter box instead of ringing our doorbell, I wouldn't have had to try and open the front door in the first place.

And my fishing clothes wouldn't have got squashed.

Mum said it wasn't the postman's fault, it was my fault. She said postmen aren't allowed to bend big letters in half, so he had to ring the doorbell.

After she'd unjammed the front

door and got the big letter from the postman, she made me take my pile of special fishing things upstairs, and put them on the end of my bed.

Not including my red bucket. 'Cos the bucket had got dirty in our shed.

That's the **trouble with our shed**. My mum is far too lazy to clean inside it.

After I'd put the bucket in the kitchen, Mum said it was time we went to the supermarket to buy all the things we'd need for our picnic. I love buying picnic things. Especially picnic things to go fishing with!

CHAPTER 10

The **trouble with supermarkets** is they're useless.

I mean, why don't they put the Scotch eggs next to the crisps?

Why don't they put the crisps next to the lemonade?

Why don't they put the lemonade next to the spicy chicken wings?

And the spicy chicken wings next to the Babybels?

I mean, why oh why oh why don't supermarkets put all the important fishingy picnic things together, under one big high-up sign that says FISHINGY PICNICS?

If I was the manager of a super market, I'd throw all the soaps and shampoos and pet food in the bin, and put all the picnic things together on one massively long giant shelf.

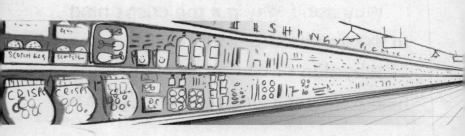

Mum said that maybe I should save up my pocket money and buy my own supermarket. Then I could put whatever I wanted on the shelves.

And I could be the supermarket manager.

And I could use the bleepy thing that they use to swipe your shopping with at the till.

I'd love to have a bleepy thing of my own. I'd bleep every single thing in my house.

Mum said if I had a bleepy thing at home she'd end up doing a few bleeps of her own!

But the **trouble with super-**

market bleepy things is there's nowhere you can buy them.

You can't even buy them in a supermarket!

When we got home with our shopping, Mum let me help her put all the picnic things into the cool box, ready for the next day!

I squeezed as many of my favourite things in as I could!!!

Once I'd filled the cool box right

to the very very top, I asked if I could put it on the end of my bed, with my clothes.

But Mum said no way.

I think she thought I would eat it all in the night, but there's no way I would have.

Not all of it anyway.

"I'll put the cool box on the kitchen

table, Daisy," she said. "Our picnic will be a lot safer there."

The **trouble with putting cool boxes in the middle of kitchen tables** is it makes you want to keep

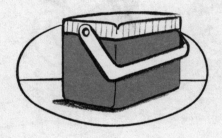

checking the picnic things inside.

You know, to see if we've forgotten anything.

Or to see if there's room for another bag of crisps.

Or a Babybel.

Or half a sausage roll.

Trouble is, I had to climb onto a kitchen chair to reach.

The **trouble with climbing on kitchen chairs to reach the lids of cool boxes** is the legs on our chairs are bit wobbly.

Mum says that's because I keep swinging backwards and forwards on them like a monkey, instead of sitting at the table like a proper little girl.

But I reckon they're badly made chairs.

The **trouble with badly made chairs** is if you stand on them, and reach and stretch, the legs start to wobble.

And if you start to wobble too, they wobble even more.

And if you wobble and stretch and lean too far . . .

A chair leg might fall off . . .

Actually, definitely will fall off.

72

Which means the chair will fall over.

And you will fall over too.

Onto the kitchen floor.

With a loud BANG CRASH!

And an OUCH!

And a CRUNCH!

Which isn't your fault.

It's the chair leg's fault. I mean, chair legs aren't meant to fall off, they're meant to stay on!

But the **trouble with chair legs** is they can't speak. So they can't own up.

So you get the blame.

When my mum found me sitting on the kitchen floor with a chair leg in my hand, she guessed what I'd been trying to reach.

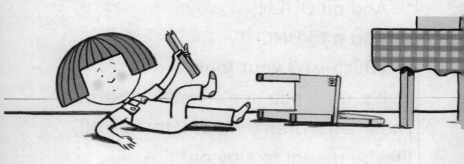

So she put the cool box right up high, on top of the kitchen cupboards! Where I could barely even see it!

Which meant I couldn't touch it until Sunday.

Or sniff it until Sunday.

Or anything it until Sunday!

Which made me cross all over again!

It made me SO cross, I did one of my special frowns, all through Saturday afternoon.

All through Saturday tea time.

All through Saturday evening, and right up to the time I had to go to bed.

WHICH WASN'T MY FAULT EITHER!

CHAPTER 11

The **trouble with seeing a pile of fishing clothes at the end of your bed** is it makes you stop being cross, but start getting really excited again instead.

Which is even more annoying.

Because then you definitely can't get to sleep on Saturday night.

Even after four bedtime stories I couldn't get to sleep.

Even after counting fish jumping over a hedge, I couldn't get to sleep.

Which is why, on Sunday morning, I woke up at quarter past two.

The **trouble with waking up at quarter past two** is it makes your

mum really grumpy if you wake her. I know because I've tried it before, at Christmas.

So I didn't wake my mum up at all. I just got dressed into my fishing clothes and went downstairs. To find the dirty bucket. The **trouble with dirty buckets** is you can't take

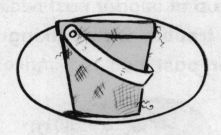

them fishing unless they're clean. Especially if you're going to put fish in them.

Because fish don't like dirt. Especially shed dirt.

Our red bucket was really really

covered in shed dirt, so I really really had to clean it at half past two in the morning. In our kitchen sink.

The **trouble with cleaning a dirty bucket at half past two in the kitchen sink** is once you've filled the bucket with water from the taps . . . you can't lift it out.

Because it's so heavy.
So you have to really really huff

and puff and lift and lift, and strain and strain, and pull and pull until . . .

Er . . .

The trouble with buckets coming out really fast is . . .

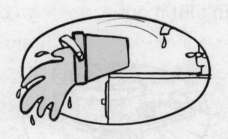

it makes you drop them . . .
Which means they splosh . . .
And splurge . . .
And sploooossshhh . . .

all over the place . . .

Which isn't your fault.

It's the bucket's fault for having a slippery handle.

Or the water's fault for being so heavy.

Luckily, none of the bucket water splashed on my fishing clothes, because I managed to jump out of the way.

Trouble is, it went all over the kitchen floor instead.

The **trouble with kitchen floors** is they're not really meant to be wet.

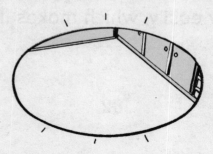

Especially at 2.30 in the morning.

Kitchen floors are meant to be dry at 2.30 in the morning.

And 2.45.

So I decided I'd try and mop it.

The **trouble with my mum's floor mop** is the handle is too long, which

makes it really awkward.

And the mop doesn't squeeze out very easily, which makes it really heavy.

Plus, the heavier it is, the harder it is to lift it up to the sink.

I thought after about three mops of the mop, all the water on the kitchen floor would be gone. But it wasn't. There was still loads of water everywhere.

Even after about five or six lots of mopping, the mop STILL hadn't worked properly and mopped all the water up.

WHICH TOTALLY ISN'T MY FAULT!

So I decided to go back to bed.

Without doing the rest of the mopping.

Trouble is, my mum woke up at quarter past three.

Double trouble is, she needed a drink of water.

Which is why she went downstairs to get one.

Which is why she walked into the kitchen in her nightie.

And in her bare feet.

The **trouble with walking into a wet kitchen with your nightie on**

and bare feet is . . .

Er . . .

It kind of makes you slip over onto your bottom . . .

And scream . . .

And, er . . .

Get a soggy bottom . . .

And soggy legs . . .

And soggy elbows . . .

Which, er . . .

Kind of . . .

Was my fault.

Which is why I pulled my bed covers over my head and pretended to be asleep.

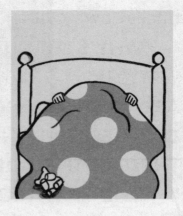

Except Mum came upstairs into my bedroom and turned my light on.

And pulled my bedcovers back.

Which meant she saw I was dressed in my fishing clothes.

Which is how she knew it was my fault that the kitchen floor was wet.

Plus I hadn't put the mop and

bucket away either.

"WHY'S THE KITCHEN FLOOR ALL WET???!" she shouted. **"AND WHY ARE YOU WEARING YOUR FISHING CLOTHES! IT'S ONLY TWENTY PAST THREE IN THE MORNING!**

"AND WHAT IS THAT FILTHY BUCKET DOING IN MY SINK!!!!!!!?"

I told you mums get grumpy if they wake up too early in the morning.

CHAPTER 12

When I got up for my breakfast, I decided to stay out of the kitchen. Which is a good job really, because the floor didn't dry out till about half past nine.

My mum didn't stop doing her own special frown until eleven o'clock either, so I was really glad when my Uncle Clive and Auntie Sue arrived to pick us up in their car.

I couldn't wait to get in Uncle Clive's car when he arrived at our house. Uncle Clive's car is much bigger than our car.

It can fit all kinds of fishing things in it, AND picnic things, PLUS four people, PLUS my red bucket too!

Except Uncle Clive said I wouldn't need the bucket, because he had a proper fishing net we could use to keep fish in instead.

So I put the bucket back in the shed. (Well, near the shed, 'cos I was in a hurry to get back to the car.)

When we got into Uncle Clive's car, Mum looked really funny. She'd stopped frowning, but her eyebrows still looked really wonky. That's because my uncle's

long green bag with the fishing rods
in was right in the way of her head.

It was so long
and so big, it
was squashing
her hair and her
earrings and
everything!

That's the **trouble with fishing
rod bags.** You have to be quite
short to sit next to them.

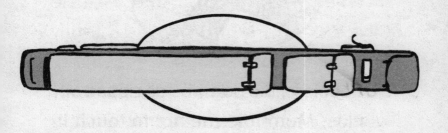

So in the end, me and my mum swapped over seats.

The **trouble with having a fishing-rod bag near the top of your head** is it's really exciting. It really makes you want to open the bag to see the fishing rods inside. Even if you're still in the car and you haven't got to the river yet.

Trouble is, the bag was all zipped up. Plus, Mum told me not to touch it.

So all I could do was feel it with my hair.

And my imagination.

When we arrived at Paper Mills lock, my hair and imagination were really beginning to ache!

When I saw the river, I nearly wet myself!

Once Uncle Clive had parked the car in the car park, we all helped to unload it. The **trouble with unloading cars** is I never get to carry any of the best bits.

I really wanted to carry Uncle Clive's great big rod bag, or his huge green box of fishing things, with a strap.

Trouble is, they were too heavy.

So I carried the picnic blanket and my hoodie instead.

The **trouble with picnic blankets** is they're really itchy. At least Auntie

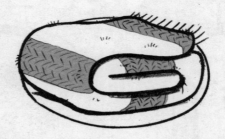

Sue's picnic blanket is. It felt a bit itchy when I first started carrying it, but by

the time we had walked past Paper Mill pool, through the gate, past the lock gates, past the café, and right up past the river boats, Auntie Sue's picnic blanket had nearly itched my arms off!

Luckily I didn't have to sit on it later because Uncle Clive had brought me a special fishing chair to sit on instead!

He showed it to me when we arrived at the place we were going to fish in. Special fishing chairs are really important when you're fishing. Because they mean you can sit really comfortably, right up close next to your fishing rod.

I know, because guess what!

Uncle Clive had brought me my own special fishing rod to fish with too!

You should have seen it!

It was even longer than me!

CHAPTER 13

The **trouble with fishing rods** is there are all kinds of different ones to choose from.

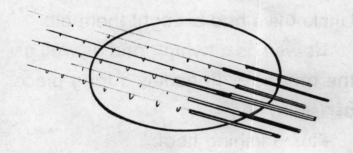

Uncle Clive says that if you haven't been fishing before, then the best type of fishing rod to start off with is a smallish one.

Smallish fishing rods are specially for beginners. They come in two pieces, but they still look quite big when you push them together.

There are lots of special things that you need to bring if you're going to go fishing for the first time. And Uncle Clive had brought them all!

As well as a "whip", and as well as the maggots, I needed a long piece of fishing line.

Plus a fishing float.

Plus a teensy little coloured rubber band.

A box of fishing weights.

And a fishing hook.

At first I didn't really know how any of the fishing things Uncle Clive had brought were meant to work. But when my mum had finished putting my sun cream on, Uncle Clive showed me how to join them all together!

It was BRILLIANT!

This is what my Uncle Clive told me I had to do:

Step One: *Push the two pieces of your fishing rod together.*

Step Two: *Put your fishing reel onto the handle of the fishing rod and make sure it's nice and tight. (I got Uncle Clive to put my reel on.)*

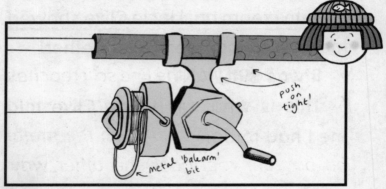

push on tight!

← metal 'balearm' bit

Step Three: *Pull the metal bit on your fishing reel back and pass your fishing line through all the little circles on your rod. (I got Uncle Clive to do mine.)*

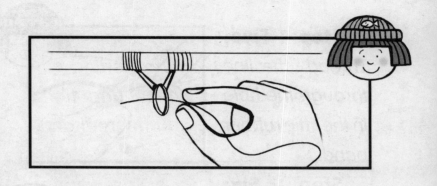

Step Four: *Pull the line so it reaches from the top of your rod right down to your knees. And then push the metal bit on your reel back the other way.*

(Uncle Clive says the metal it is called a "bale arm". I got him to do the bale arm bit too!)

Step Five: _Thread the line through the hole in the little rubber band._

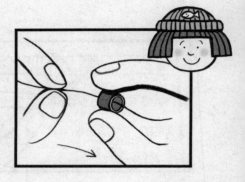

Step Six: _Push the fishing float through the rubber band too, then thread the end of the line through the circle at the bottom of the float. (I did all the other steps_

by myself!)

Step Seven: *Now the float is on, slide it up the line with your fingers.*

Step Eight:

Tie a hook to the line, using a really really good knot. (I got Uncle Clive to tie my hook knot too.)

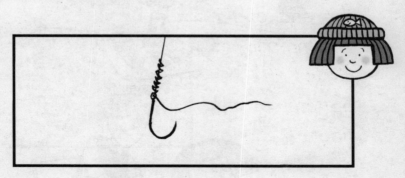

Step Nine: *Pinch the right amount of fishing weights onto the line with your fingers.*

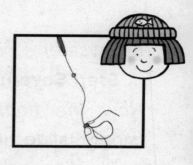

Step Ten: THEN GET READY FOR THE MAGGOTS!

CHAPTER 14

Maggots! Wriggly tiggly maggots!!!

At first when Uncle Clive took the lid off the bait box to show them to me, I thought, NO WAY!!!!!! There is NO WAY I'm touching a maggot!!!!!!!!!!

When my mum and Auntie Sue saw them, they nearly dropped their glasses of white wine!

Mum said that maggots were the most disgusting things on earth. She said they were filthy, and horrible, and yuk!

But after I'd watched them wriggling around in the bait box for a while, I realized they weren't filthy at all.

Or horrible.

Or yuk.

They were just maggots.

And actually, they looked quite clean.

Uncle Clive said that when you buy a pint of

maggots from a fishing shop, they put sawdust in the bait box to keep them comfy.

Maggots love sawdust. And really hot sunshine.

Really hot sunshine makes maggots wriggle even more.

In fact it makes them about the wriggliest tiggliest things in the world.

After about two looks, I started to really like them. In fact I was thinking about taking one home to be my pet.

But Uncle Clive said that it wasn't a very good idea to get too attached to a maggot. He said the only thing that should get attached to a maggot is a hook.

The **trouble with hooks** is I'd never put a maggot on one before.

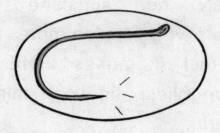

In fact I'd never even picked a maggot up.

So Uncle Clive showed me how to do it.

Actually, he picked the maggot up for me, and then put it in the palm of my hand. The **trouble with having a maggot in the palm of your hand** is, well, at first you want to drop it. Because you think it's going to wriggle and tiggle all over you.

But actually, it doesn't feel that wriggly tiggly at all. If you make your hand into a cup shape, it just wriggles around in your palm really lightly, and stays there without you even hardly feeling it at all.

Which is really neat!

Uncle Clive showed me that there are two ends to a maggot.  There's a thin end. And there's a fat end. The fat end has two tiny dots on it, like eyes, except they're not, and the thin end has got a little black line inside it, like a brain, except it isn't.

It's the fat end that you have to put the hook in.

Once I'd done that, it was time to cast my fishing rod out!

CHAPTER 15

The **trouble with casting fishing rods out** is it takes lots of practice.

If you don't pull your metal bit back before you do it, the fishing line won't come off your reel, plus if you let go of the line at the wrong time, you might get into a tangle. I reckon you might even hook yourself up the nose with a maggot!

Uncle Clive said that the best thing would be for him to cast out for me. He said the more I watched him do it, the more I would see how to do it.

So I let Uncle Clive do my casting out for me.

You should have seen how good he was at doing it! He got my float to land in just the right place, every single time! Even his first cast went in exactly the right place.

All I had to do was sit in my special chair and wait for a nibble!

The **trouble with nibbles** is

I thought I was going to get one straight away. Except I didn't.

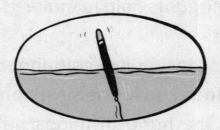

Uncle Clive said that there is one other important thing you need when you go fishing, and it's called patience.

Patience means waiting for a fish to bite your maggot.

Uncle Clive said that we were in a really good fishing place, but we might have to wait a while for the fish to get hungry.

Then he threw some extra maggots into the water right next to my float. Extra maggots help to make fish extra hungry.

Then Uncle Clive said that he was going to set up his new rod, and once I'd got the hang of things he would cast out a maggot too. Then we would have two chances of catching a fish instead of one!

Uncle Clive's new rod was different to mine. It had an actual fishing reel on its handle, with loads of line and everything.

That's because Uncle Clive is a fishing expert. He knows how to do fishing reels and everything.

And he knows how to do rod rests!

Rod rests are rests for your rod. Uncle Clive pushed two into the ground, right beside my seat, and then showed me how to rest my rod on them.

"There you go, Daisy," he said. "You're all set up. Now sit tight and watch your float. And remember, if your float goes under, it means you've got a bite!"

So I did sit tight. I sat in my special fishing chair with my rod on my rod rests and I looked at my float, and I waited.

And waited.

And waited.

For at least about three minutes.

The **trouble with waiting waiting and waiting for at least about**

three minutes is it really makes you want a sausage roll.

So I asked my mum if I could have one.

And she said I could! As long as I cleaned my hands first with a wet-wipe.

So I did! And it was yummy!

(Not the wet-wipe. The sausage roll.)

The **trouble with eating a sausage roll** is it makes you want to have a Scotch egg.

So I asked my mum if I could have

one of those too!

And she said I could!

So I did! And it was yummy too! Especially the yellow bit in the middle.

The **trouble with having a Scotch egg after you've had a sausage roll** is it makes you want to have a jam tart.

So I asked my mum if I could have one of those too.

And guess what! She said I could!

I told you picnics were great fun, didn't I!

Except then I got really really thirsty.

So I asked my mum if I could have a glass of cherryade too!

And she said I could.

But I had to come and get it myself.

So I didn't.

Because I couldn't.

Because I was fishing!

That's the **trouble with mums on picnics.**

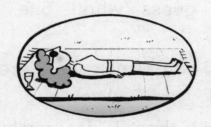

Picnics make them even lazier. They're so lazy they can't even get up off the picnic blanket and walk about two steps across the grass to give you a drink of cherryade. Even if you really really need one.

Luckily Auntie Sue brought me some cherryade instead. Otherwise I'd probably have died of thirst.

The **trouble with cherryade** is it's really wet.

Especially if you drop it in your lap.

It wasn't my fault I dropped my

cherryade in my lap. Or over my trainers. It was my uncle's fault.

He was the one who shouted "STRIKE, DAISY!" not me.

The **trouble with someone shouting "STRIKE, DAISY!"** is if you don't know what "STRIKE, DAISY!" means, you don't know what to do.

So I just jumped. And dropped my cherryade.

While Mum was wet-wiping the

stickyness off my jeans, Uncle Clive told me that while I was looking at my cherryade my fishing float had gone under.

Which means I'd had my first nibble!

Trouble is, I wasn't looking at my float when it happened. I was looking at my cherryade instead.

Which is why Uncle Clive shouted "Strike, Daisy!"

"Strike, Daisy!" means: "Pick up your rod quickly, Daisy, and lift it up into the air! Or the fish will get away!"

Not: "Drop your cherryade in your lap, Daisy, and all down your legs."

Which is what I did.

At first I was a bit embarrassed.

But Uncle Clive said not to worry. He said everyone misses their first bite and he was sure the fish would come back and nibble my maggot again.

And guess what.

He was right!

CHAPTER 16

The next time my float went under, I WAS watching!

I saw the yellow tip of my fishing float bob up and down a little bit first, and then jiggle a bit more, and then disappear right out of sight under the water!

When I lifted my whip off the rod rests and raised it up into the air, I

could feel an actual alive fish tugging on the end!!!

It was so exciting!!!!!

When I lifted the fish out of the water, I could see how big it was and everything.

It was about seven or eight centimetres long AT LEAST. It was a silvery-green-coloured fish with red fins, and when my uncle took it off the hook, he told me it was called a roach!

Roaches are the best!

Uncle Clive put my roach into a great big long round net and dropped it into in the water in front of us. He said we would keep all the fish that

we caught in the net and then let them go at the end of the day.

Which was even more exciting, because then it was like catching pets, because they couldn't swim away!

Then Uncle Clive showed me how sucked the maggot was!

The **trouble with sucked maggots** is they can't wriggle. Even if you

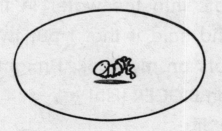

hold them up in the sunshine, they

can't wriggle.

That's because all their wriggle juices have been sucked out by the fish.

The maggot didn't look at all wriggly any more. It looked like a sucked-out empty bit of sausage skin.

So I had to throw it away.

While I was throwing it away, Uncle Clive threw some more extra maggots into the water in front of me, and said if that I put two new maggots on my hook, I might catch an even BIGGER fish!

So I did!

And guess what!

I caught a skimmer bream!

And then guess what!
I caught a dace!

So now we had THREE fish

swimming in our net!

How exciting is that!

AND THEN . . . you'll never guess this . . .

And then, absolutely GUESS WHAT!

Uncle Clive let me throw a whole handful of maggots into the water ON MY OWN!

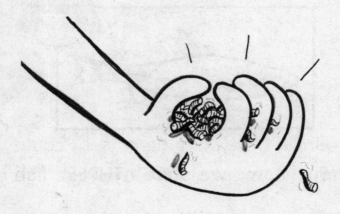

He let me stick my actual fingers inside the actual bait box and put about a hundred maggots in my hand all at once!!!!!!!!

The **trouble with throwing about a hundred maggots all at once** is it's harder than it looks. Especially if you have to land them near your fishing float.

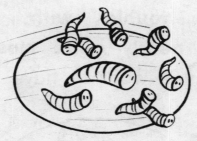

Uncle Clive said the closer I could land the maggots to my float, the more chance I would have of getting another nibble.

Trouble is, my first throw went closer to my trainers than my float!

Uncle Clive didn't mind. In fact he laughed, and told me to have another throw!

So I did! And this time I got almost nearly quite close!

The **trouble with getting almost nearly quite close** is it makes you want to have another

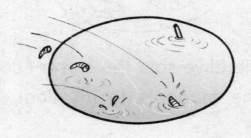

throw to see if you can get almost nearly quite closer.

Uncle Clive said that we had plenty of maggots in the bait box, and another throw would be fine.

So I did have another throw!

And this time I got totally almost absolutely quite nearish!

By about my sixth throw, one of my maggots hit my float!

That's when Uncle Clive said he thought I had thrown enough maggots into the water.

He said if you throw TOO many maggots in when you're fishing, the fish will get full up, and stop biting.

My arm was aching anyway after about five throws, so I sat back down in my chair and waited for another bite.

Uncle Clive said I'd definitely got the hang of fishing now, so he was

going to cast his rod out too.
So now we were BOTH fishing!
HOW EXCELLENT IS THAT!

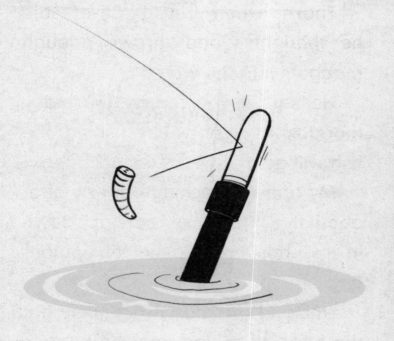

CHAPTER 17

You should have seen how far my uncle could make his float go!

It went right across the river and nearly touched the river boats that were parked on the other side!

Uncle Clive said that sometimes fish liked to hide under river boats, and that if he could get his bait really close, he might catch a big one.

Trouble is, every time a river boat went past us, he had to keep reeling his line in.

That's the **trouble with river**

boats. If your fishing line gets run over by a river boat, you'll end up in the worst type of fishing tangle ever!

Uncle Clive said he was used to fishing boats driving past him, because he'd fished Paper Mill river lots of times before.

So there was no need to worry.

Then guess what!

I caught another roach!!

Trouble is, it had swallowed my maggot so much, I couldn't see the hook!

When I looked inside its mouth, I couldn't even see my maggot!

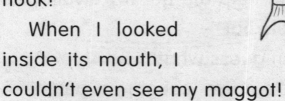

Luckily Uncle Clive had a special fishing thing called a disgorger.

A disgorger is a long thin metal thing that takes swallowed hooks out of fishes without hurting them.

Uncle Clive said everyone who goes fishing should learn to use a disgorger. Except I didn't need to be able to use one yet, because he was there to help me get my swallowed maggots out.

Then guess what!

Uncle Clive caught a perch! A wopping great big perch that was almost as big as his hand!

Perch are really beautiful. They've got black stripes down their bodies, and a great big spiky fin on top of their backs!

Uncle Clive said you have to be careful when you pick up a perch, just in case you get prickled. That's why I let him drop it into the keep net instead of me.

Fishing with Uncle Clive was the best! We had the best maggots, the best fishing rods, the best picnic, and the best place in the whole world to fish in.

And then it got even better!

It got all messy and squidgy and

mucky and fun!!!
   Because now we were mixing up
GROUNDBAIT!

CHAPTER 18

At first when Uncle Clive filled a tub with water from the river, I thought he was going to throw it over my mum and Auntie Sue.

I don't know why I thought that, because I don't think they would have been very pleased. Especially as they were sunbathing.

I'm glad I was wrong anyway, because instead of throwing the tub of river water over my mum and auntie, Uncle Clive carried it over to me and put it on the grass.

"If you bring your rod out of the water for a little while," he said, "I'll show you how to mix up some groundbait!"

Groundbait is special balls of breadcrumbs that you throw into the water.

Like bombs!

You can throw them like bombs for miles!

And they make really big splashes when they land in the water!!

Uncle Clive says that fish who live near the bottom of rivers love eating groundbait. Especially groundbait with maggots in!

This is my recipe for making groundbait bombs with maggots in! I've called it *Maggot Surprise:*

Step One: *Take one big tub of river water. (Get someone to help you fill it, or you might fall in.)*

Step Two: *Slowly pour in the breadcrumbs from a great big bag of dried*

groundbait. (You can buy the bag in a fishing shop.)

Step Three:
Swish the dried breadcrumbs around in the river water with your fingers!

That's right.

Your actual fingers!

Step Four: *Pour some more dried breadcrumbs in, and then squidge the river water*

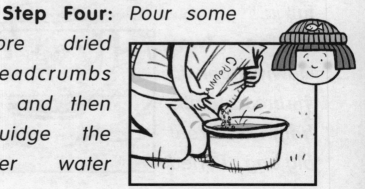

into the mixture some more with your actual fingers.

Step Five: Keep pouring and mixing and squidging more dried breadcrumbs in, until the mixture goes all nice and yukky and then a bit stiff.

Step Six: Sprinkle a great big handful of maggots in and mix them into the mixture with your actual fingers too!

Step Seven:

Take two big crumbly handfuls of stiff mixture and  squash them into a round ball. The bigger the ball, the bigger the bomb. The bigger the bomb, the bigger the splash!

Step Eight:

Wipe your hands on your T-shirt. And on your jeans if your fingers are still sticky.

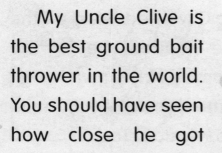

My Uncle Clive is the best ground bait thrower in the world. You should have seen how close he got when he threw his bombs at his float!

And you should have seen how excited the ducks got when they saw all the splashes!

Uncle Clive said the ducks would eat all the groundbait before the fish if they got a chance. Trouble is, groundbait bombs sink to the bottom really fast, so to reach them, they'd need beaks about as long as my rod!

Once Uncle Clive had used all the groundbait he needed, he let me make some bombs of my own.

And he let me throw them in quite almost near to my float too.

I made one big bomb, three little bombs, two medium bombs and five bullets.

Then I threw them in!

You should have seen the splashes. And heard the kerploops when they landed in the water!

Mum said she reckoned all the splashes and kerploops we were making with our bombs and bullets would frighten all the fish away.

But Mum doesn't really understand fishing. Plus she's nowhere near as good at fishing as me.

Uncle Clive said that once the fish on the bottom of the river found out where our groundbait had landed, they'd be hungrier than ever.

And guess what!

He was right!

CHAPTER 19

First of all I caught another roach. And then I caught another dace. And then I caught a different type of fish called a gudgeon, and then I caught a perch too!

It wasn't as big as my uncle's perch, but I still let him take it off the hook. (In case it tried to prickle me.)

Mum and Auntie Sue were really impressed. In fact they were so impressed at how good I was, they opened another bottle of wine! And poured me another cherryade!

And they let me finish off the cheesy puffs!

The **trouble with cheesy puffs** is they're too crunchy to put on a hook.

I reckon if I liked cheesy puffs so

much, fish would like them to eat too, even if cheesy puffs don't wriggle.

But Uncle Clive said that maggots were definitely the best bait to use. He said now that the fish were feeding, all we had to do was KEEP them feeding.

He said if we could keep the fish feeding, we would be catching fish ALL AFTERNOON!

Then guess what he did!

He opened his big fishing box with the strap on, and took out something even better than maggots and groundbait and worms!

He took out his fishing catapult!

The **trouble with fishing catapults** is unless you've seen one before, you don't really know what they do.

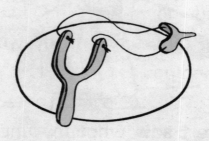

Or how they work.

But you definitely know they're really interesting. Even if you haven't held one before.

I was so interested in my uncle's fishing catapult, I forgot to ask for a chocolate mousse!

Once I saw what my uncle Clive could do with his fishing catapult, my eyes nearly popped out of my head!

Fishing catapults are BRILLIANT!

THEY CAN MAKE MAGGOTS GO FOR MILES!!!!

I reckon if you pulled the elastic on

a fishing catapult back a really really long way, you could ping maggots right into space!

You could probably land some on the moon!

This is what my uncle's fishing catapult looks like.

And this is how he made it work!

Step One: *He held the catapult handle in one hand.*

Step Two: *He filled the pouch with maggots.*

Step Three: *He lifted the handle and the pouch carefully, making sure the maggots didn't fall out.*

Step Four: *He put his pinging finger though the loop on the pouch.*

Step Five: *He pointed the handle up in the air.*

Step Six: *He pulled the pouch back with his pinging finger.*

Step Seven: *He made the elastic stretch and stretch and stretch . . .*

Step Eight: *He let go with his pinging finger and . . .*

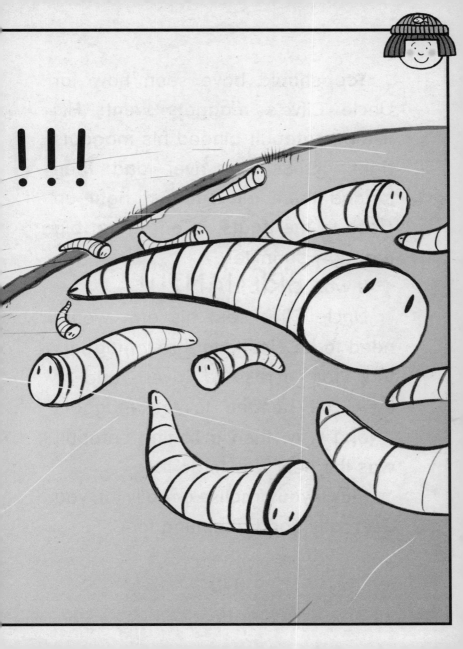

You should have seen how far Uncle Clive's maggots went! His fishing catapult pinged his maggots right across the river and then landed them all together, right up close to the boats, in one great big maggoty sprinkle!

It was BRILLIANT!!!

Uncle Clive said his arm would need to be elastic to throw maggots that far across a river, and if ever you needed to fire maggots a long way, then a fishing catapult was the best way to do it.

Plus if you practise a really lot, you get really good at aiming too.

Uncle Clive is SOOOOO clever! He can ping maggots right across a river, right up close to his float, EVERY SINGLE TIME!

Which made me really really want to have a go with the fishing catapult too.

So I asked him if I could.

AND GUESS WHAT!

He said YES!

ACTUAL YES!

CAN YOU BELIEVE IT?

I never believed fishing could get this much fun! I was catching loads of fish, I was touching actual maggots with my actual fingers, I'd made actual bombs out of actual groundbait, and now I was going to get to ping actual maggots a really long actual way with an actual fishing catapult!

Plus, as long as I remembered to wipe my hands with a wet-wipe first, I could have as many cheesy puffs as I wanted in between pings!

And sandwiches!

And Scotch eggs!

And cherryade!

It was BRILLIANT BRILLIANT BRILLIANT!!!!

After about seven practice pings I was an expert at eating cheesy puffs and pinging fishing catapults all at the same time!

In about six seconds I could wet-wipe my fingers, fit three cheesy puffs in my mouth and fire about twenty maggots nearly almost half-way across the river!

And nearly almost always landed my maggots where I was aiming!!!

One of my best pings nearly even landed some maggots on a duck!

Going fishing with Uncle Clive and Auntie Sue and my mum was the BEST thing I'd ever done in my WHOLE LIFE!

It was fabbo!

It was whizzo!

It was brillo!

Until Jack Beechwhistle and Harry Bayliss came along in their canoes.

CHAPTER 20

Why did Jack Beechwhistle and Harry Bayliss have to come canoeing up the river? Just when I was really enjoying myself, just when I was getting really good at fishing, and just when I'd forgotten about all those whopping great fibs they'd been telling me ALL WEEK, they had to come paddling up the river near to me.

At first I didn't even notice them. I was so busy pinging my maggots at my float that I didn't see them coming at all.

It was only when my uncle wound his rod in that I looked up the river to see what was coming towards us.

First time I looked, all I could see was a great big long line of canoes, paddling up from the lock gates. In the front canoe there was a man with a whistle in his mouth, and behind him were children learning how to paddle.

Everyone was wearing puffy orange life jackets and crash helmets, which made their faces harder to see.

Second time I looked, I spotted Jack and Harry right at the back of the line.

The **trouble with seeing Jack Beechwhistle and Harry Bayliss at**

the back of a canoe line is it makes you really cross.

It makes you forget all about fishing, and cheesy puffs, and Scotch eggs and picnics, and it makes you think about ALL THE FISHING FIBS THAT THEY'VE BEEN TELLING. . .

AND TELLING AND TELLING AND TELLING . . .

ALL WEEK!!

My Uncle Clive reeled his fishing

line right in and said , it was "sunshine and sandwich time". Then he went and lay down on the picnic blanket next to my mum and Auntie Sue.

But I didn't.

I stayed in my special fishing seat and watched the canoes.

Especially the canoes at the back.

The **trouble with watching canoes at the back** is they're really annoying.

Especially if they've got Jack Beechwhistle and Harry Bayliss inside them.

At first I wasn't sure if they had

seen me.

But when they stuck their tongues out, I knew they had.

The **trouble with sticking your tongue out at me** is you really shouldn't do it.

Especially if I'm doing one of my special frowns.

And triple especially if I've got a fishing catapult in my hand.

The **trouble with me doing a special frown AND having a fishing catapult in my hand** is it means you're gonna get pinged. . .

BIG TIME!!!

CHAPTER 21

This is how I pinged Jack Beech-whistle and Harry Bayliss with my fishing catapult!

Step One: *I slowly lowered my fishing catapult, so that they wouldn't notice it.*

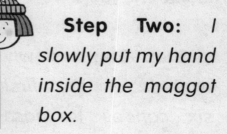

Step Two: *I slowly put my hand inside the maggot box.*

Step Three: *I slowly got a great big handful of maggots.*

Step Four: *I slowly put the maggots into the pouch.*

Step Five: *I slowly put my ping finger inside the loop.*

Step Six: *I slowly waited for the first six canoes to pass by in front of me.*

Step Seven: *Then I quickly lifted up my catapult,* pulled back my ping finger and . . .

BLAM!

I pinged Jack Beechwhistle and Harry Bayliss

all over with maggots!

It was brilliant! Jack Beechwhistle tried to duck out of the way, but Harry had never seen a catapult before, so he didn't even know what I was doing!

By the time he realized he'd been sprinkled with maggots, I'd pinged maggots all over him again! It was so funny!

Jack   Beechwhistle   tried   to

paddle away really fast, but then he remembered he was the second-best canoe expert, and his job was to stay at the back, behind Harry.

Which meant he had to come back for more!

I was laughing so much when I pinged him the third time, I nearly fell off my seat!

Then my uncle sat up to see what I was doing.

At first I thought he'd be really cross, but when I told him I'd pinged Jack and Harry by accident, he told me to be more careful, and laid back down on the picnic blanket!

Which meant I could try and ping them with maggots again!

Trouble is, they were out of range now, so my maggots wouldn't reach.

After he'd paddled past me, Jack Beechwhistle looked back and tried to splash water at me with his paddle.

But he missed by miles!

Then he stuck his tongue out even further! And he crossed his eyes!

I stuck my tongue out as far as I possibly could! And I called him a Canoe Face.

192

Which serves him right. Because it was him and Harry who started it. Not me. If him and Harry hadn't told me all those fibs about fishing, then I wouldn't have pinged maggots at them at all.

I might even have waved nicely at them instead. I might even have pinged them some cheesy puffs.

But I didn't.

I pinged the big fat fibbers with big fat maggots instead.

WHICH WAS TOTALLY THEIR FAULT!

CHAPTER 22

The **trouble with pinging Jack and Harry with maggots** is it really makes you want to ping them again. Even though you know you really shouldn't.

And especially if your uncle has told you not to.

Trouble was, Jack Beechwhistle

and Harry Bayliss had paddled too far down the river for me to reach them, so I couldn't ping them again anyway.

Which meant I had to think of something else to aim at instead.

First of all I looked at my float. But I'd already aimed at that before.

Then I aimed at my keep net. But that was too easy to hit.

Then I aimed at a dragonfly. But it wouldn't stop darting around.

So I had no choice really.

I had to aim at some river air instead.

The **trouble with aiming at river air** is sometimes an actual river boat can get in the actual way.

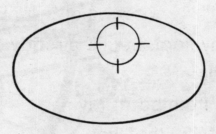

Especially if the sun is shining in your eyes at the same time that you ping the maggots out of your catapult.

That's exactly what kind of happened to me.

Can you believe it! Just as I fired at this really small piece of river air, a river boat sailed straight past in front of it!

And the sun really came out, straight in my eyes.

Which meant my maggots missed the river air I was aiming at, and hit the river boat in front of me instead.

The **trouble with accidentally pinging maggots into a river boat is** the people on the boat might be having a picnic as well.

Which means your maggots might
end up in their picnic basket.
Or in their cups of tea.
Without them noticing . . .
. . . at first.

The **trouble with noticing there's a maggot in your cup of tea** is it makes ladies on boats scream really loudly.

And spit their tea out into the river.

Which makes your uncle sit up.
And your auntie.
And your mum.

The **trouble with seeing maggots in ladies' hair** is it makes men on

boats shout quite loudly too.

Especially if the ladies are freaking out.

Which makes your mum, auntie and uncle get up off the picnic blanket and stare right across the river. And then at me.

At first I thought I'd pretend I was too busy fishing to notice. That way, they wouldn't know the maggot-pinger was me.

But when the man on the boat threw the whole tray of cakes into the river (including the tray), I decided I'd better try and hide the catapult fast.

The **trouble with trying to hide a catapult fast** is the only place I could think to put it was up my stripy T-shirt.

Trouble is, it made my tummy bulge. Plus my uncle saw me hide it there. Which wasn't good.

But before he could say anything, there was a really loud scream from up the river.

Which wasn't good either.

Then there were some really really

loud whistles from up the river too.

Which made things even worser.

And then the river boat I'd pinged maggots at crashed into the bank beside us.

Which made things terrible.

And then the whistles up the river got even louder and LOUDER and **LOUDER!**

Which was really bad news, because we weren't the only ones who could hear them. After about twelve really loud whistles even the people in the cafe by the lock gates had run up the river to see what was happening.

Uncle Clive didn't know whether to run up the river towards the whistles, or help the people who had crashed their boat right beside us.

I did. I ran up the river as fast as I could with Auntie Sue and my mum. Except that when I saw where the whistles were coming from, I kind of wished I'd stayed in my seat.

Right in the middle of river, Jack Beechwhistle and Harry Bayliss had dropped their paddles and were doing really really fast kayak rolls. At first I thought they were practising, but after about six rolls I realized

that they were the only children
who were doing them.

Plus every time the man with the whistle told them to stop, they just kept doing another turbo-spin upside down and under the water again.

Double plus, each time their faces came up out of the water, their eyes went kind of bulgy and their lips kind of squealed like the ladies on the boat, like something was freaking them out too.

Which meant . . .

er . . .

I was in even bigger trouble now.

The **trouble with having maggots in your pants** is they're really hard to get out. Especially if your legs are wedged inside a canoe.

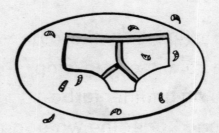

That's what had happened to Harry and Jack. Some of my maggots had gone down the necks of their life jackets, and crawled right down their backs and into their undies!! They hadn't realized until they were further down the river!

Which meant there was nothing that Harry and Jack could do!

Except freak!

Plus roll over and over and over in the water, every time they felt a maggot wriggle round their bottoms!

215

Which was really really funny!

Everyone felt really sorry for them, but I thought it was HILARIOUS!

In the end, four grown-ups had to dive in, otherwise they'd still be spinning round and round in the water now!

After Harry and Jack had been got out of their canoes, they had to take their trousers down to shake the maggots out of their pants.

I even saw their bare bottoms! It was so funny!

Trouble is, then Jack told everyone that the maggots had been pinged by me.

Which wasn't funny at all.

Double trouble is, then Uncle Clive arrived with the people who had crashed their boat. Plus a strawberry cheesecake with maggots all over it.

So then I had to own up to everything.

Which got me into something my mum called "really deep water". Which means really big trouble, without getting wet.

As from today, I am officially banned from pinging anything with a catapult ever again.

Plus I'm not allowed cheesy puffs or cherryade in my picnics ever again. (Mum says the E-numbers drive me off the rails.)

Plus, can you believe it, I'm banned from fishing with Uncle Clive for a whole month!

That's four weeks and two whole days!!

CHAPTER 23

The **trouble with being banned from going fishing again for FOUR WHOLE WEEKS AND TWO WHOLE DAYS** is it makes you even crosser!

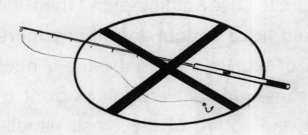

I mean, just when I was getting really good at fishing and pinging, Jack Beechwhistle and Harry Bayliss had to come along in their canoes and spoil everything.

If I hadn't been made to pack all my fishing gear away by my mum, I reckon I'd have caught an even bigger dace or roach yesterday afternoon! I'd probably have caught a bigger fish than my Uncle Clive!

Uncle Clive said he didn't think we would have caught very many more fish at all. He said that once a boat crashes into a riverbank in front of you, the sound of the crash usually frightens all the fish away.

Fish don't eat very much when they're frightened.

Plus we only had two maggots

left in our bait box. I'd pinged all the others into the river.

In the car on the way home, Uncle Clive said that I shouldn't be cross, I should be reflective.

Trouble is, I don't know what reflective means, so I'm going to stay cross instead.

Just like my mum.

Mum says that pinging maggots at people in boats is an absolutely disgusting thing to do, and if she'd known Uncle Clive was going to let me ping maggots all over the place, she wouldn't have let me go fishing in the first place.

And she wouldn't have let me have any cheesy puffs either.

When I got to school this morning, Jack Beechwhistle and Harry Bayliss were waiting outside the school gates yet again. Except this time they had their mums with them too.

So I got into even MORE trouble.

Jack Beechwhistle's mum said that Jack and Harry might have nearly drowned when the maggots wriggled into their pants, and that firing missiles at children in canoes was a very naughty thing to do.

Oh well, at least I saw their bare botties! They won't be telling me any more fibs after that!

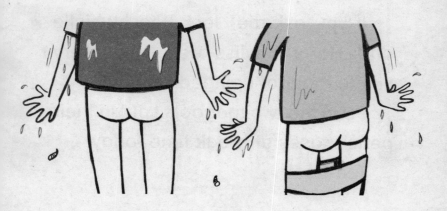

Plus Harry Bayliss doesn't need any more kayak-roll practice now either. In fact, thanks to me, Harry and Jack Beechwhistle are now the two best kayak-rollers in the world!

I'm really really glad I went fishing with my Uncle Clive. It was sooo much fun! Even if I did get told off. And even if I am banned from fishing. And catapults. And cheesy puffs. And cherryade.

If you ask me, Jack Beechwhistle and Harry Bayliss deserved every single maggot I pinged at them.

PLUS the two maggots I put in their pencil cases at break time today!

Tee-hee!

DAISY'S TROUBLE INDEX

The trouble with . . .

 Maggots 3

 New fishing rods 8

 Asking my mum if she wants to go fishing 9

 River boats 11

 Jack Beechwhistle 12

 Harry Bayliss 19

 Paper Mill lock 23

 Kayak rolls 26

 Killer whales 32

Seeing a pile of fishing clothes at the end of your bed 76

 Waking up at quarter past two 77

 Dirty buckets 78

 Cleaning a dirty bucket at half past two in the kitchen sink 79

 Buckets coming out 80

 Kitchen floors 81

 My mum's floor mop 82

 Walking into a wet kitchen with your nightie on and bare feet 85

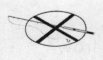